THE MORAL OF THE STORY

and

THE LAST HERO

by

Jerry Patterson

THE INTERNATIONAL UNIVERSITY PRESS
INDEPENDENCE, MISSOURI 64055
1987

ISBN 0-89697-311-5   LCN 87-092120

MORAL OF THE STORY

A One Act Play by

JERRY PATTERSON

Dedicated to Bill Mays

PROPERTY PLOT

Scene One

Double bed
Chair beside the bed
Chest of drawers
Dresser
Bedside table

Scene Two

STRIKE above.
Desk
Desk chairs (two)
Certificates, plaques on wall
Ash tray
Optional props on desk.

Scenes Three, Four, Five

STRIKE above.
Sofa
Easy chairs
Coffee table
Desk and Typewriter
Desk chair

CAST
(in order of appearance)

GEORGE WILLIAMS   Successful, middle-aged novelist.

THE VISITOR   A vision with preternatural qualities.

EDWARD TRAUTMAN   New York publisher.

MARILYN KIRKPATRICK   George's friend and neighbor.

DON WILLIAMS   George's son, a Princeton senior.

SYNOPSIS OF SCENES

SCENE 1: George's Bedroom.

SCENE 2:   Office of Trautman Publishers in New York.

SCENE 3: Living room of George's apartment.

SCENE 4:   Same.

SCENE 5:   Same.

SCENE ONE

SCENE:
> *Apartment bedroom of novelist George Williams, located near the East River in New York. The room is tastefully furnished in contemporary, yet masculine style.*

AT RISE:
> *It is approximately 2:00 a.m.*
> *GEORGE, a tall, graying blonde-haired man of medium build, wearing pajamas, is aroused from his sleep when he hears a voice calling his name. He awakes to find a man of medium size and build comfortably seated in a chair beside the king-sized bed.*
> *The unexpected visitor is dressed in a beige business suit, striped shirt, and dark brown necktie. He wears heavy horn-rimmed glasses which seem to hide or distort his facial features.*

VISITOR
(leaning slightly forward toward George's bed, but remaining seated)
> George! George, old man.
(George reacts)
> No need for alarm. I apologize for this impromptu, if not rude,awakening in the middle of the night, but we really have some things to muse over between us; subjects that can often be broached best at this time of night and under present conditions of awareness.

GEORGE
(sitting up in bed confused though not frightened by the intruding apparition)
> Who are you, and how did you get inside my bedroom? If you aren't a real man, then this is the most realistic dream I've ever experienced. Still, you seem to have some sort of glow within you that illuminates the

5

room. You couldn't be an angel, could you? My faculties seem too alert for me to be dead.

VISITOR
(chuckling in order to put his confused host at ease)
No, George, nothing so dramatic, nor traumatic as that. You're very much alive and in complete control of all your faculties as you suggest. You might call me something of your 'alter ego' for want of a better label. "Conscience" is such a banality these days and "Id" is just too strong a term for my sensitivities. Why not just call my your "Visitor," George? That seems a convenient term which avoids emotional or clinical overtones.

GEORGE
(moving to edge of the bed and placing both feet on the floor)
Well, 'Visitor,' now that you have invaded the privacy of my bedroom and awakened me in the middle of the night, just what matters must we consider that cannot be held in abeyance until a more reasonable time and place?

VISITOR
(crossing his legs and leaning back comfortably in the chair)
Well, George, I think we best begin by considering your last novel. Sales went very well on the first publication, but did you really feel good about this particular work?

GEORGE
I always feel good when I add to my bank account and the reviews on the book are better than average.

VISITOR
It was a commercial success all right, George. I won't deny as much. However, let's look at some other

aspects of our life. You've been pretty self-centered of late, haven't you? I don't mean just as a writer, but as a man. Why have you isolated yourself so much during the past year? Your work schedule hasn't demanded it.

GEORGE
Well, my divorce had a lot to do with it, I suppose. Since splitting up with Ellen, I've been moody, temperamental, and generally incompatible. According to her, I was all of those things before the divorce as well. (rising)
Funny that you called me self-centered a minute ago. Ellen referred to me as being 'selfish' from time to time. I was 'selfish' because I was too busy writing and trying to make a living for us to show her proper attention, I suppose. Well, there are some positive things that can be said for being selfish. If you always watch out for yourself, you won't have to depend on others to do it for you. If everyone looked out exclusively for himself, then at least we'd have a world full of self-reliant people. (sitting)
I'm selfish enough not to marry again. I'm convinced that's the prudent course for me.

VISITOR
Maybe your wife had a point. You seem to admit the allegations yourself.

GEORGE
(rising to face VISITOR directly)
Look, my benign intruder, I don't hurt anybody else in my isolation do I? I made a generous property settlement and am supporting two overprivileged young adults who are my children and I think that's a pretty fair record.

VISITOR

No, you don't hurt anyone, nor do you do anything to help anyone either, George. Your splendid isolation extends to all human commitments, doesn't it?

GEORGE
(moving left toward Visitor)

Yes, I guess it does, but that's my work style. My profession is a lonely one. A writer has to isolate himself if he wants to accomplish anything. I make an occasional party now and then. That's enough involvement for me.

VISITOR
(rising)

Let's look at another facet of your lack of involvement. You were reared in a church-going home and active yourself right up through college. Remember how involved you were in all the youth programs? Every Sunday night you'd be down there in the church basement leading the discussion groups and trying to get your friends to help you build the kind of society you visualized. Sort of lost the vision somewhere along the way, eh, George?

GEORGE

I can't tell whether you're the ghost of my past, or a store-front psychiatrist on a misguided house call. (sitting at foot of bed)

Yes, I was once involved in church activities, but that was when I was a kid. It was all part of middle-class Middle American culture. I haven't attended church much since I was in college. We sent the kids to Sunday School when they were young, but that was the extent of our involvement. Maybe later when I have more time, I might become active in the church again. Right now I need to concentrate on creative writing. I can contribute more to mankind by producing books than thumping them behind a pew or podium. Besides, the social utopia I expected simply will never exist – at least not in this world.

VISITOR
(moving toward GEORGE)
Possibly, but let's look at the record thus far. The protagonist of your last novel was a rather aggressive sort, wouldn't you say? He loved money and power and promiscuous sex and managed, rather successfully, to obtain all three. How much good for mankind can a novel with such a character really do?

GEORGE
That character still had redeeming virtues. He wasn't completely selfish and he paid the price for what he got from life.

VISITOR
Sure. Voluntarily broke off a relation with his nineteen- year old mistress after growing tired of her. Real self- sacrificing type. (sits down in chair)
The hero in the manuscript you're currently working on seems to be cut largely from the same bolt of cloth.

GEORGE
You're a moral snob, my friend. and a rather clairvoyant one at that.
(rising)
Aggressiveness in pursuit of wealth and power is admired by a large portion of the world – especially the American reading public – if not by the churches. I write about human beings in my novels, not plaster saints! (moving right)
No one would read those books if the heroes were simply 'goodie-goodies' right out of the Junior Patriot series. The reader wants a fellow human being with whom he can identify in a novel. I try for an ethic in my stories all right, but writing, or any other art for for that matter, is not just a matter of moralizing.

VISITOR
The Bible has done pretty well throughout the years.

GEORGE
(moving to center)
But I'm not competing with the Bible. I'm writing for the leisure market and for contemporary tastes. Do you expect me to come up with a modern 'Paradise Lost' in my next manuscript? Today's reader is just not interested in moral preachment from an author. Even the 'muckrakers' have pretty well had their day.

VISITOR
(leaning forward in chair)
Nevertheless, George, great societies do produce great literature and the reading public buys what's published.

GEORGE
Exactly, 'Visitor,' and I want to publish great novels. (sits on edge of bed)

VISITOR
More writers should share your aspirations it not your example. Look at the state of publishing in the United States today. The newsstands rival the restroom walls of a city bus station. The films are even worse. One can barely take the family to a movie today without being saturated with obscene language, blood mania, and candid, or even kinky, sex.

GEORGE
Yes, I know. One more film about the traumas of being a homosexual and I'm ready to privately boycott the entire industry. But getting back to my

novels, I don't resort to vulgar sensationalism; only realism.

VISITOR
(rising)
Yes, but sometimes that realism looks a lot more like commercialism, George. Are your novels really contributing to making the world a better place?

GEORGE
Visitor, with each comment you're sounding more like a preacher.

VISITOR
Speaking of preaching, George, remember how at age fourteen you wanted to be a minister? Ever regret not becoming one?

GEORGE
Not really. I wouldn't have been a good one. Ministers are constantly moving from place to place and once the idealistic glamour of the profession wears off it becomes a dull and prosaic life.

VISITOR
Yes, material things and personal ego became more important along the way didn't they?
(moving right toward GEORGE)

GEORGE
Well, it's only human to want things like money, recognition, and admiration from one's peers isn't it?

VISITOR
Of course, you're only normal in that respect, George, and most people are not capable of becoming successful clergymen. Still, don't you miss contact with the church at all? At least you'd meet some members

of the congregation who'd serve as character models for your novels.

GEORGE
        Yes, but does attending church on Sunday really make me a better man the following week?

VISITOR
(sitting beside GEORGE on bed)
        No guarantee that it will, but compare those who practice a formal religion with those who don't and see which group is more moral. The results are pretty obvious, regardless of whether we consider individuals or entire societies.

GEORGE
        Yes, but the results will also depend a great deal on who's conducting the survey.
VISITOR
(rising)
        George, I have to be going now. I let the time slip up on me as most of us do. We need to talk again soon. Some day we all have to account for how we spent our time and talents on this old globe and it's something you ought to seriously think about. Be seeing you, George. (exits left)

GEORGE
(rising from the bed and following left)
        What I just experienced could not have been a dream – at least no ordinary dream. That man's impact was just too realistic to be ignored.

CURTAIN.

SCENE TWO

SCENE

One month later George is seated in the office of EDWARD TRAUTMAN, Managing Editor of Trautman Publishing Company, a New York-based publisher. TRAUTMAN is seated at his desk opposite George.

He is in his middle fifties with a sober and business-like countenance. He is wearing an Oxford shirt and solid-colored tie.

The office is expensively, but not pretensiously, furnished.

TRAUTMAN

As always, George, your characterizations are clear and well-developed, but your protagonist in this manuscript seems to moralize a bit too much. Somehow he comes off weak. Is he suppose to be intimidated by women? This 'wimp' is a far cry from Clint Martin in your last novel whose vividly describe life-style made the book very readable.

GEORGE

I hear you, Ed, but in retrospect I'm concerned that Clint Martin's life-style may have been a bit too romantic. His extra-marital affairs could have an adverse influence on readers.

TRAUTMAN

George, the people who buy your novels are looking for entertainment, not a manual on how to conduct an affair. We're not publishing Sunday school bulletins, either. I publish books about flesh-and-blood-type characters with whom a reader can identify. If those characters have human character flaws, then so do the people who read about them. I can't be 'my brother's keeper' for every individual who reads a book with the Trautman trademark on it, can I?

GEORGE

Possibly not, Ed, but certainly we owe some social responsibility to the reader – at least I as an author do. Novels can and have changed the course of history and anyone who calls upon the muse shouldn't forget it.

TRAUTMAN
(fumbling for a cigarette and offering same to George who declines)

Why this sudden social responsibility awareness, George? Do you have a guilt feeling? Do you believe someone had an adulterous love affair because of something one of our fictional characters did within the confines of a book? These issues have never disturbed your writing before. (lights cigarette)

Now you seem suddenly prudish.

GEORGE

Not prudish, Ed, just more aware than I have been in the past. Maybe you could say that I'm beginning to consider myself my brother's keeper.

TRAUTMAN

Well, I can't argue with you over your own reactions, George, but from a publisher's standpoint this manuscript is just not up to your usual standard.
(thumbs pages of the manuscript casually)

Now, I can make some suggestions for making the title character a bit more exciting, but they'll have to do with the commercial aspects of the story, not its moral influence.

GEORGE
(rising)

Thanks for the offer, Ed, but I believe I know what you're going to suggest and I'm afraid I like the character as I created him. Don't think I'm being unappreciative, but let me consider some changes on my own and then we'll talk about our ideas and the manuscript one day next week. I'll call you and set up the appointment about Monday.

TRAUTMAN
(rising)
        Suit yourself, George. You know how much this publishing house values you as an author. We want you to keep turning out good commercial novels for us, so don't let your conscience crowd the muse too much.
(smiles and extends his hand to George)

GEORGE
(shakes hands with Trautman and smiles reluctantly)
        We'll be in touch, Ed, and thanks for your offer.
(exits right)

(Trautman returns to desk and sits down. Shakes head to express slight confusion.)

SCENE THREE

SCENE:
Two days later. Living room of George's apartment where he is being visited by MARILYN KIRKPATRICK, a neighbor. The room is furnished in good contemporary taste.

Marilyn is a widow and an analyst with a New York brokerage firm. She is approximately forty years old, slender, with reddish-brown hair, blue eyes, and sweet smile.

She is wearing custom-style jeans and a white sweater.

AT RISE:
George, dressed casually in slacks and a sport shirt, is seated beside her on the couch and sipping a cup of coffee. George has related cautiously, and somewhat reluctantly, to Marilyn his experience with the 'Visitor' last month and the influence it has had on his subsequent writing.

MARILYN
No, George, I don't think you're crazy, nor eccentric after hearing your story. Plenty of normal, trustworthy people have reported experiences similar to yours. With your fertile writer's imagination, I would guess that you had a very realistic dream in which you had pretty serious dialogue with your own conscience. That's all. Probably everyone should have those introspective discussions every now and then.

GEORGE

Well, thanks for reassuring me that I don't belong in the looney bin, Marilyn, and I believe your theory about a dream is probably correct. However, since that occurrence – whatever it may have been – I've taken a very different view of my work and even of my life. Not a comfortable view either.

MARILYN
Elaborate if you will, George.

GEORGE
(setting cup on table in front of couch)
Well, in retrospect my writing seems a profitable activity for me which has provided an interesting diversion for many other people. On the other hand, none of my books have contributed to making a better society, nor even inspired a single individual reader to lead a better life. In fact, they have probably had a negative influence on the collective morals of my readers.

MARILYN
Being a bit harsh with yourself, aren't you?

GEORGE
(leaning back and facing Marilyn)
No, pretty objective. Just as the characters in my novels have aggressively sought power, money, and joys of unrestrained sex, my own life has been an egocentric pursuit of materialism and pleasure. I can't see that I've had much of a social conscience for the past twenty years and I've had no contact with organized religion or any other charitable institution. Since my 'experience,' I've been very aware of the fact and uncomfortably so at that.

MARILYN
You could well be missing out on something, George.

GEORGE
Do you to church regularly, Marilyn?

MARILYN

Yes, I do, George. I've been a fairly regular church-goer all my life. However, I've been a lot more involved since Paul's death than I was previously. I'd like to be even more active because church work has filled a definite need in my life and a void as well. I've gotten to know some truly fine people in our congregation.

GEORGE

I'm sure you must have.

MARILYN

George, why don't you go with me to church this Sunday? I believe you'll like the minister and I've known you long enough to ask you for a date, haven't I? (laughs)

Besides, your self-diagnosis sounds to me as though you'd make a fine member of our congregation.

GEORGE

Maybe I'll just do that, Marilyn. I can hardly remember when I last attended church services, but it might be good therapy for my 'middle-age blues' and guilt feelings.

Besides you certainly propose an inexpensive date and I insist upon providing the transportation.

MARILYN

It's a deal, George. I believe you'll be taking a giant step in the right direction.

GEORGE

(rising and reaching for Marilyn's empty cup)

Let me give you some more coffee, Marilyn.

MARILYN
(rising)
No more just now, thanks, George. Really must be running. Besides, you probably want to get back to work.

GEORGE
Even with my ambivalent feelings about my current manuscript, I suppose I should.

MARILYN
(exiting to the left)
See you on Sunday, if not before, George.

GEORGE
It's a date, Marilyn.

CURTAIN.

SCENE FOUR

SCENE:
> *Same. Three months later. It is the middle of a Friday afternoon.*

AT RISE:
> *George is at his typewriter when he hears a knock at the door.*

GEORGE
(rising to answer door)
> Okay, coming.

(opens door and greets son, DON, a Princeton senior, who is paying an impromptu call)

(Don looks a great deal like George, but is slightly taller and more slender.)

DON
> Hi, Dad.

GEORGE
(extending right hand to shake hands)
> Well, Don. This is a pleasant surprise. What brings you up to the big city?

DON
> Cindy and I came up for the weekend. We're staying with Mom at the house, but I thought I'd drop by and say hello to you while we're still en route. Hope you'll pardon me for not phoning first.

GEORGE
> Of course. It's a nuisance to have to stop and telephone from the turnpikes. Much better to just 'pop in' as you did. Come on and sit down. Get you anything to drink?

DON
    No, thanks, Dad.
(sitting in easy chair)
    Not just now. Cindy's waiting in the car, so this will have to be a quick drop-in and drop-out.

GEORGE
(sitting on couch opposite Don)
    Well, wish you'd brought Cindy up, but then I know the fast pace of an Ivy Leaguer's holiday in New York. I'm sure you're on a tight schedule tomorrow, but I'd like to take you and Cindy to lunch on Sunday. In fact, why don't the two of you plan to go to church with Marilyn, my down-the-hall neighbor, and me and then we'll dine immediately after?

DON
    Wish we could, Dad, but we have to start back early Sunday morning. Have to be back on the campus by noon. However, next time I'm in the city I'll take you up on the offer of staying here with you for a few days. Also, I'll let you know the graduation schedule as soon as it's firmed up.

GEORGE
    That'll be great, son. I'm looking forward to a few days at the alma mater with the sons of old Nassau. Sorry not to be able to take the two of you to church, however. You would really like the pastor, Dr. McIntyre.

DON
    I'm sure we would, Dad. You mentioned him in your last letter, but frankly I was a bit surprised at your sudden involvement in the church. You and mom always sent Sue and me to Sunday School, but I can't remember the two of you ever being especially active in religious affairs.

GEORGE
Unfortunately, we weren't, Don. But we should have been. Would have been better for you and Sue and might have saved your mother's and my marriage.

DON
Do you really think so?

GEORGE
(nodding slightly)
Yes, I do.

DON
(nodding, in response and looking at the door)
Well, church sounds like a good outlet for you. In your last letter you mentioned that you're now teaching a Sunday School class, I believe.

GEORGE
Temporary substitute teacher at the moment, but will have my own class in a couple of months. Really a pleasant experience for me, too, Don. I believe I enjoy teaching those classes more than writing novels.

DON
Great but there must be quite a disparity in income from the two activities.

GEORGE
True, but then 'man shall not live by bread alone,' shall he? Seriously, Don, do you attend chapel services on campus very regularly?

DON
Not too often, Dad. Right now, I'm pretty busy with my course work plus applying for several law schools and boning up for the admissions exams.

GEORGE
The admissions exam is next month, isn't it?

DON
Three weeks from tomorrow, as a matter of fact. My grades are good enough for acceptance just about anywhere, but I figure I'll still have to score in the ninetieth percentile or better to have my pick among Harvard, Columbia, and Yale.

GEORGE
I figure those three schools will all be clamoring for you, Don. Getting back to chapel services, I wish you'd get in the habit of attending. Don't make the same mistake that your mother and I did and ignore the influence of religion in your life. I don't know Cindy's religious preference, but if the two of you marry, then let the church be an integral part of that marriage. Don't wait until you're at my stage in life before you realize what you've ignored.

DON
Thanks for the advice, Dad; attending chapel services now and then certainly wouldn't hurt me, but it will be some time before Cindy and I think about marriage. Several other hurdles to be cleared first. What about you, though? How is work going on the present novel?

GEORGE
(rising and moving left toward typewriter)
Well, not too good to be honest with you, Don. I've tried to inject a moral message into the story and now the publisher thinks I've created a protagonist who's too much of a 'goody-goody.' Ed Trautman won't publish the manuscript the way it now reads.

DON

I'm sorry to hear that, Dad. Do you think you can make the necessary revisions in order to get published?

GEORGE
(picking up manuscript from desk and rubbing it against his left palm)

I'm not so sure, Don. It would be easier to try and find another publisher, but I'd probably meet the same objections all over town. I'm taking a different approach to writing just now and it's going to mean a loss of dollars for me I fear.

DON

Yes, and I can imagine all the time and effort that you've put into that manuscript. (lights a cigarette)

Just what is this new approach to writing that you're embarking on, Dad?

GEORGE
(moving right toward Don)

Basically, Don, I want to write books that will have a more exemplary influence on readers. My work in the future will have to be more socially responsible -- more morally responsible, if you will. I'm through writing junk that focuses on the amoral hedonism and power struggles of the American upper-middle-class. However, I will have to accept that my income will be less if I write for a less commercial market.

DON
(rising to get an ashtray)

Dad, I wouldn't call your novels 'junk,' nor would any competent literary critic. However, if you're sending me a message about reduced financial power, then I don't have to enroll in the most expensive law school in America. Even if I do, I can rely on my own resources. I don't want to saddle you with heavier financial burdens.

GEORGE

Hold on a minute, Don. You're getting way ahead of me. I didn't say I was 'broke,' did I? I want you to go to the best law school that accepts you. You want to practice with a top Wall Street firm you said. Well, we both know those firms won't even look at your resume unless you graduate from one of three or four Eastern law schools.

That's your goal and I intend to see that it's fulfilled. Just keep in mind that material success and even the prestige and recognition that go with it are not the only reasons for living.

DON

I'm sure that's true, Dad, but then I've never lived without the benefits of material comforts and neither have you for that matter. (sits down in chair)

If I can speak candidly for a minute, I'm a bit confused about your sudden religious zeal. I don't doubt your sincerity, but this apparent guilt feeling coupled with self-examination, if not deprecation, is very unlike the 'you' I've known all my life. It seems sort of, well – unsophisticated for you. (laughs)

Next, you'll be giving testimony as a 'Born Again Christian' and championing some itinerant evangelist.

GEORGE
(sitting on edge of the couch)

Well, in a sense, I have been 'born again', or maybe reoriented by outside influences, Don, but the lack of sophistication in these experiences doesn't mean a lack of validity. Don't worry, I won't become some sort of impractical mystic in a hair shirt.

25

DON
(smiling)
I'm sure you won't, Dad, and I admire your integrity. (puts out cigarette)
Really can't keep Cindy waiting any longer. (rising)
Better get downstairs. Nice seeing you, Dad, and sorry that the visit had to be so brief.

GEORGE
(rising to shake hands with Don)
Appreciate your taking the time to stop and see me, son. I'll look forward to your graduation, and remember there's always plenty of room for you here in the apartment any time you're in town. Keep me informed on law school acceptance.

DON
(moving left to exit)
Will do, Dad, and remember I don't want law school to be a monetary problem for you. With Sue starting to college this fall and the other financial obligations you already have, I want you to consider my expenses a low priority.

GEORGE
On a flaming pair of stilts, I will, son! You'll go to the law school of your choice and you'll go first-class. I never worked a day while I was in college and you won't either. Getting through the academic grind and competitive pressures of a prestige law school's 'paper chase' is enough to absorb any man's full energies. I don't want you to have to 'grub' for money as well. Just don't forget that there's more to life than being a rich Wall Street lawyer.

DON
Don't worry, Dad. I'll ring you up one evening next week. (exits)

GEORGE

Right, son. Careful of the traffic this time of day.
I love you. (directed toward Don as he exits and
descends the stairs. Pauses and then walks back to
couch and sits)

He's right about my financial situation. Sue is all
set on enrolling in Smith this fall and expects to be
there for the next four years. Seeing Don through three
years at Harvard Law School won't be exactly a credit to
petty cash. The divorce lowered my working capital
while increasing monthly rental costs and now I
suddenly decide to drastically cut my own income.
Would be better for my dependents if I cut my own
throat. Maybe I should go ahead and let Ed Trautman
publish the story the way he wants it. After all, my first
obligation is to my own children, isn't it? Why should
they sacrifice because of my perceived responsibility to
society? I've got to provide the money somehow. (bows
head)

Dear God, let me know what approach to take. I
need your advice.

CURTAIN.

SCENE FIVE

SCENE:
Two months later. Living room of George's apartment. He is dressed casually and is closing a cardboard packing crate when the doorbell rings.

GEORGE
(moving toward the door)
Coming.
(opens the door to find Marilyn standing outside)

(She is wearing slacks and a sweatshirt.)

Marilyn, greetings! Come in! Come in!

MARILYN
Thanks, George. (enters living room)
You don't waste any time once you make a decision, do you? I wanted to offer my services in helping you pack, but looks as though you're already well underway in that project.

GEORGE
As a matter of fact, I am. Can I offer you something to drink, notwithstanding all glasses and cups are tightly packed away?

MARILYN
Oh, no. Thanks anyway, George. Would be easier for you to come over and sip something with me when you are at a good breaking point.

GEORGE

Good idea. That should be in about ten minutes. Sit down, Marilyn. Please.

MARILYN

Thanks. (takes a seat on the couch)
Sure I'm not interfering with your packing?

GEORGE

Never. I'm just on the verge of stopping. I've packed just about everything except a few last-minute items which I'll cram into the big box over here just before the movers arrive in the morning.

MARILYN

I'm going to miss you as a neighbor, George. Really hate to see you leave the building, but hope you like your new place.

GEORGE
(sitting beside Marilyn on couch)

I'll miss you as a neighbor as well, Marilyn, and I don't expect to like the new place as much as I do this one. It's just barely above the tenement class. Well, sort of ranging between delapidated brownstone and the cold water flats of the Village, but I'll make out okay.

MARILYN

I'm sure you will, George.

GEORGE

Several things to tell you since I last saw you, Marilyn. Don called last night. He's been accepted to Harvard Law School and is pretty sure it will be his choice for the fall.

MARILYN
That's wonderful, George. Aren't you proud to have such a brainy son?

GEORGE
I am. He'll make a fine Wall Street lawyer. I just hope a good ethical, Christian one. You know, he didn't even embarrass me by bringing up the subject of my finances or asking how much I'll save on rent at my new address. On the positive side, he feels pretty confident that he'll get some sort of minor, but carte blanche, scholarship through the alumni association. I didn't know he was applying, but that kind of aid could hardly come at a better time for me.

MARILYN
I knew things would work out, George, and I'm pleased for you and Don both.

GEORGE
So am I, Marilyn, but that's not all the good news. My manuscript is now in the hands of a literary agent who believes he can sell it without revision to a smaller publisher here in the city. Of course, there probably won't be an advance and I won't realize anything comparable to the money I would have made had Trautman published it, but at least I stand to get some much-needed income for months of work that would otherwise go down the drain.

MARILYN
Much better that it go for paying tuitions at Harvard and Smith, eh?

GEORGE
I'll say! So by cutting down on my monthly rental expenses and invading my tax sheltered savings, I should be able to survive the next few years okay, even

if I'm not knocking out a best seller every twelve
months.

MARILYN
        But you do intend to keep writing, don't you,
George?

GEORGE
        Yes, of course, but in a very different vein.
Here's the best news of all. Yesterday afternoon, I
interviewed the Editor-in-Chief of the Asbury
Publishing House just across the river. Next month I
will be working as an assigned writer for them and I'm
truly looking forward to it.

MARILYN
        George, that's terrific. Things are really working
out for you this week.

GEORGE
        St. Paul promised me as much as nineteen
hundred years ago, Marilyn, and somebody's prayers got
through to the top.

MARILYN
        Indeed!   The job sounds very interesting,
George, and with good, steady work you won't be
concerned over financial security.

GEORGE
        Well, I doubt that I'll ever be living in the six-
figure income bracket again, Marilyn, but I don't
foresee my family having to make any financial
sacrifice. I'll miss the material comfort that I've grown
so fond of through the years. There's no point in trying
to kid myself or anyone else on that point, but what's
even more important, I'll be creating characters of
whom I'll be proud and who might influence real
people's lives for the better.

MARILYN

George, I'm really proud of you. Know your 'visitor' of a few months ago would be proud as well.

GEORGE

Guess I'm even proud of myself for the first time in a long time, Marilyn. It's too late for me to revert to my adolescent goal of becoming a minister, but I can at least dedicate my typewriter and imagination to promoting Christianity so long as I can hit the keys and have something to say in so doing.

MARILYN

(leaning forward and kissing George on the cheek)

Nobody is happier for you than I am, George, with Dr. McIntyre likely to run a close second. I want you to come over for dinner this Saturday evening so we can celebrate all this good fortune that's come your way. Think you'll be moved in and settled down enough in the new bailiwick by then to resume your social life?

GEORGE

You bet I will, Marilyn, but only on the condition that you go with me to Princeton for Don's graduation in two weeks.

MARILYN

It's a date.

GEORGE

(rising)

Great! You'll never know what a benign influence you've had on me during the past few months, Marilyn. I hope I can repay you in some way.

MARILYN
(rising)
You've already begun, George. Now let's take a
little break from your packing chores and toast your
new career.

CURTAIN.

"THE LAST HERO"

A One Act Play

by Jerry Patterson

To:
The memory of Fred Livingston, Jr.

-FOREWORD-

In a mythical country in the western hemisphere sometime during the twentieth century, a civil war has just taken place. Leftist rebel forces overthrew the civil government and forced the President into exile,only to be defeated by a coalition led by General of the Army John Willhart. Martial law and a military dictatorship have been established by General Willhart who has now assumed the title of Military Governor of the nation.

Although defeated in battle, the leftist forces still pose a threat to the order and stability which Willhart feels he must maintain in governing the nation.

CAST   *[in order of appearance]*

GENERAL JOHN WILLHART (Military Governor)
WILLIAM COOPER (Political Ally)
JOSEPH LANE (Leader of the Liberal Party)
HUMAN LIBERTIES ASSOCIATION SPEAKER
SEVEN LISTENERS (Male and/or female)
POLICEMAN NO. 1
POLICEMAN NO. 2
ANNOUNCER
ELIZABETH WILLHART (Wife of General Willhart)
GENERAL JAMES CROWLEY (Willhart's First Deputy)

SYNOPSIS OF SCENES

Scene 1 - Willhart's Office.
Scene 2 - The same. One year later.
Scene 3 - A city street. One month later.
Scene 4 - Government mansion. Two weeks
    later.
Scene 5 - The same. Several hours later that
    morning.

PROPERTY PLOT
(Scenes One and Two)

Desk.
Leather easy chair.
Desk chair.
Several diplomas, certificates, and plaques on wall.
Ash tray on desk.
Optional props on desk.

(Scene Three)

STRIKE above.
Elevated speaker's platform.

(Scenes Four and Five)

STRIKE above.
Sofa.
Two sitting chairs.
Briefcase.

SCENE ONE

: Office of GENERAL JOHN WILLHART, Military Governor of a mythical country in the western hemisphere, sometime during the twentieth century. It is a fairly large room, but of Spartan furnishings to include desk, easy chair, and some diplomas and plaques on the wall behind the desk.

AT RISE:

GENERAL WILLHART is seated at a large mahogany desk, UL, which faces diagonally toward down center. He is a tall, well-built man in his mid-forties and is wearing a dress uniform.

WILLIAM COOPER, friend and political ally, is standing by a leather chair, UC, and to the right of General Willhart's desk. He is a tall, slender, gray-haired man, approximately fifty years old. He is wearing glasses and a dark three-piece suit.

COOPER
(standing in front of Willhart's desk)
Well, General, the war is over now and you're a national hero. Looks as though the power is all concentrated on our shoulders for the time being.

WILLHART
Yes, I guess I can interpret the title of Military Governor about any way I choose, can't I?

COOPER
(taking a seat beside Willhart's desk)
Seems the people are willing to grant you absolute power, John -- at least until we can get things organized once more. You earned yourself quite a reputation as a military commander.

WILLHART
That's very satisfying to hear, Bill.
(leaning forward with elbows on desk)
The war was an agonizing experience for me. I could never again stomach seeing my own countrymen blown to bits by my orders. Yet, I admit that the experience of leading a combat army to complete victory was an even more fulfilling experience than I ever imagined.
(leaning back)
I love power more than ever now and the responsibility that goes with it. Guess that's why I became a military man in the first place. It's a unique feeling, Bill, to be credited with saving the nation.

COOPER
Don't get too fond of power, John. We've an obligation to hold elections as soon as possible.

WILLHART
Yes, but let's not be in any hurry with elections, Bill. We've got enough chaos to straighten out now without getting the whole nation involved. Elections and demagogues behind them were the cause of the war in the first place.
(rises and removes blouse)

COOPER
I can't deny that, John, but the people should have a voice in our reconstruction policies. We don't want them calling you a military dictator.

WILLHART
Well, some sort of label will emerge, Bill, regardless of what I do.
(places blouse on desk chair; moves to left of desk)

No, I don't aspire to be a tyrant, nor a satrap, but I do intend to see that there's order and stability in this nation.

(sits on left corner of desk)

I've been thinking a lot about popular sovereignty this past week. Democracy in this nation has meant only trouble for the past one hundred years. It's resulted in popular, mediocre men in positions of leadership because they appealed to the mob. A million ignorant "have nots" won't establish wise government through the magic of the ballot box. They haven't in the past; they won't in the future. Read history, Bill!

COOPER
(leans forward in chair)

Speaking of history, John, you might reflect a bit on the life of Julius Caesar. Sounds as though you are preparing to cross your own Rubicon and march right into a trap that you're building for yourself. The days of Caesar, Napoleon, and Alexander the Great are over.

WILLHART

I'm only asking for support, Bill, not an Emperor's crown. I have no intention of enslaving this society.

COOPER

Speaking of slavery, John, what are your plans for the emancipation of the million or so who are part of that institution just now?

WILLHART
(rising and facing Cooper)

My proposal is that slaves who want to be free will be so within one year from the date of the armistice. Their owners will be compensated fairly by the government through special manumission court. There will be a condition to this freedom, however. The former slaves will be required to leave the country and relocate in the nations of their ancestry, or some other nation willing to accept them as immigrants. We'll do all possible in assisting them in assimilating into the countries with whom we can arrange immigration agreements.

COOPER
(rising)
Good God John! You can't force them out of this country. They were born here and, along with several generations before them, have contributed to our national growth just as has the free population. They've earned the right to live here and to banish them now would be calloused insanity. They've been expecting freedom for several years, but now you propose to add that they'll be exiled the minute they taste that long-sought-after freedom.

WILLHART
(crosses to Cooper)
Bill, I don't want citizens of this nation, nor their descendants, marked by the stigma of slavery. I don't want future generations carrying a "chip on the shoulder" for what our ancestors allegedly did to their ancestors. My proposal is that either they migrate or remain in their present status as slaves.

COOPER
You mean you are unwilling to grant freedom for slaves unless one accepts banishment?

WILLHART
That's right. They'll have the alternative of remaining in slavery with their present owner if they choose not to leave the country. However, it will be the government through a commissioner of cabinet rank who will regulate the conditions of their service, not the slave owners themselves.

(sits on edge of desk)

COOPER
(moves toward Willhart)
No legislative assembly will go along with that plan, John. We'd be the laughingstock of the civilized world if we perpetuated slavery under those conditions. You know that as well as I do.

WILLHART
We'll see. I want no stigmatized, no divisive elements within this nation so long as I have the power to prevent it.

COOPER
Then be prepared for trouble, John, if that's the course you set for yourself.
(moves toward DC)
Next question: How soon do you intend to reduce the size of the military? Supporting so large an army as we now have is quite a drain on the treasury, isn't it?

WILLHART
(rising and moving toward C)
Yes, a military force is expensive for the government, but this is no time to think of reducing the size of the army. Right now, we need the security that only arms can bring until we get a stable government established.

COOPER
John, the more you elaborate on your plans, the more they sound like the foundation for a police state. The longer you keep such a strong army at your disposal, the less confidence you can expect from the citizens.

WILLHART
(places right hand on Cooper's shoulder)

Listen, Bill, no government can protect a single citizen unless it can first protect itself. There are still plenty of discordant elements out there in the streets ready to upturn things the minute we lower our defences. I don't intend to give them that chance.

COOPER

John, the people are afraid of a concentrated military force in times of peace. Surround yourself with a strong army and you won't have their support.

WILLHART
(removes hand from Copper's shoulder)

Reduce it and I won't be in power long enough to benefit from anybody's support. Bill, we've just finished fighting a civil war. We've seen one political regeime wiped out because it tried to please all factions and ignore the realities of military strength. I found myself in a power vacuum and I capitalized on it. Now, I won't drop my guard until I hear a clear bell ending the bout.

COOPER

John, you're a hell of a fine general and the nation does owe you a debt of gratitude for ending the fighting, but you're too hungry for power for yourself.
(moves left and sits on right arm of chair)

Hold back elections and hang on to slavery and you'll have another rebellion on your hands. The people don't want a Cromwell or a Caesar.
(rises)

You're setting up a military dictatorship and I want no part of it.

WILLHART
(crosses back behind desk)

You shouldn't make such a quick judgement, Bill.

COOPER
John, I can't accept your offer to be Minister of Internal Affairs in your new government, even if it's only a temporary one. I'm grateful for the opportunity, but I can't follow in the direction you intend to lead the nation.
(moves toward Willhart and extends right hand as the two men shake hands)
I wish you well.

WILLHART
(continuing to grasp Cooper's hand)
Sorry not to have you in my cabinet, Bill. I was relying on you a great deal, but I respect your decision. All the best.

(COOPER exits to right. He walks slowly, but deliberately. WILLHART watches his exit and then seats himself behind desk)

CURTAIN

END SCENE ONE

SCENE TWO

SCENE:
Same setting - one year later.

AT RISE:
JOSEPH LANE, National Chairman of the Liberal Party enters Willhart's office from Stage right. He is approximately forty years old, average size, and somewhat scholarly in manner. He is dressed in a business suit.

LANE
(extending right hand to shake hands with Willhart)
Governor, it's good to see you again.

WILLHART
(shakes hands)
Come in, Mr. Lane.
(indicating chair)
Have a seat, please.

LANE
(sits in chair beside Willhart's desk)
Thank you. I want to congratulate you on your economic program. The economy is burgeoning and we are closer than ever to full employment. How you did it without resorting to large government expenditures is amazing to me. Even your rationing program was acceptable to the people.

WILLHART
(crossing behind desk and sitting in desk chair)
The people will accept anything that is presented to them properly, Mr. Lane. We've done all we can to create an environment favorable to businessmen and

manufacturers. Without support of the capitalist class, no government can be very effective. That's why I concentrated on aid to businessmen rather than creating a public works program. I hope to reduce unemployment to the zero level within the next year. I see full employment as the only long-range deterrent toward crime.

LANE
Speaking of such, our low crime rate is the envy of the western hemisphere. You've certainly created an orderly society, Governor.

WILLHART
That was my primary objective, Mr. Lane.

LANE
(leaning forward toward Willhart)
Yet, there's another side of the issue, Governor Willhart. Along with the order and stability, there's a great deal of police power in your administration. Many are criticizing you for giving the military too much authority.

WILLHART
(rising to straighten plaque on wall diagonally behind desk chair)
I'm aware of those criticisms, Mr. Lane. There always will be some who will call any government with an efficient army a military dictatorship.
(turns to face Lane)
Of course, the Communists don't like the way I run things and never have.

LANE
(rising)
Yes, but many who are not Communists think your police forces are a bit too diligent. Don't you think that they over react at times against dissenters?

14

WILLHART
No government can survive acts of treason without fighting back. Criminals get what they ask for and if that's over-reaction, then I'm guilty of it.
(sits in desk chair)

LANE
Possibly, but there are other criticisms as well.
(sits)
You're also being called a censor, a book burner, and even the "Grand Inquisitor".

WILLHART
(leans forward with both hands grasping desk)
Yes, we've burned some pornographic literature and revolutionary propaganda. Is anyone being harmed by having such mental poison out of circulation?

LANE
It does deprive society of free circulation and exchange of ideas.

WILLHART
(leans back in chair)
Then let them circulate their pornographic trash privately and exchange treasonous ideas in prison. If the government can regulate the food its citizens eat, the water they drink, and the air they breathe, then why not the matter that enters their minds? We try to prevent air pollution in this society, so why not "mind pollution" as well?

LANE
(rising)
Regulating matter of mental consumption is not so simple as regulating matter of physical consumption.

The mind and the stomach are two very different organs.

WILLHART

Perhaps, but we still don't allow a few citizens the right to poison the air for their own enjoyment, do we?
(rising)

I won't allow any smut merchant the right to make a public showcase of books designed for sexual deviates while I have the power to prevent it. Let them exchange their "instruction manuals" in their own bedrooms if they must.

LANE

A classic argument for Comstockery, sir. Don't you believe that one should have at least the right to decide for himself what he reads?

WILLHART

To some degree, but what about the less mature or less sophisticated members of society?
(crossing to center)

Do we let our children decide for themselves what they will eat or drink? Whether or not they will attend school? Why then let obscene literature destroy a mind or malicious lies a society?
(faces Lane)

Great societies produce great literature and degenerate societies produce degenerate literature. I intend to see that ours stands in the ranks of the former, not the latter.

LANE

Yes, and propaganda can also replace much good literature with such an approach.
(sits on arm of chair)

WILLHART
Possibly more "provocative" than "good" literature, Mr. Lane. Ideas are followed by action. Books and speeches have brought on unnecessary war. Revolutions have occurred because a pack of lies or half-truths found a publisher.
(crossing back and sitting on edge of desk)
I don't want to see it happen here.

LANE
(removes package of cigarettes from pocket)
Of course you don't, but you may be encouraging it unwittingly by your own policies. Getting back to the subject of crime, Governor, some aspects of your new penal code seem to range from Puritanical to medieval.

WILLHART
Such as?

LANE
For example, the penal statutes concerning prostitution.
(rises to offer cigarette to Willhart who declines)
Public corporal punishment of convicted prostitutes strikes many people as even more archaic than ducking stools and pillories.
(takes cigarette from package)
Physically whipping these girls in the town squares promotes a morbid spectator sport. It's becoming more of a cruel form of entertainment than a deterrent toward crime.
(lights cigarette)

WILLHART
(rising)
Hard cases make good law, Mr. Lane. A leather strap across these girls' backsides is just what they need. The humiliation of having such administered in public is

17

part of the punishment, or "entertainment", as you call it. We've humiliated the streetwalkers and we've reduced venereal disease. It's damn hard to find one plying her trade in any of our cities today. Our approach has worked a lot better than fines and suspended sentence under local governments ever did.

LANE
    Next you'll be using the same solution for union organizers, I suppose.
(moves to right of chair)
    Why the recent executive order prohibiting unions?

WILLHART
(moves toward Lane)
    Because labor unions' main contribution in this country have been crime, corruption, and protection of inefficient workmanship. A National Labor Board can represent the workers' interest as well as any union.

LANE
    So the workers will now be deprived of their rights of assembly and collective bargaining? Governor Willhart, you are on the way toward depriving our citizens of all their civil liberties.
(moves to use ash tray on desk)
    People do have some individual privileges.
(turning to face Willhart directly)
    All men are born with certain inalienable rights.

WILLHART
    Men are not born at all, Mr. Lane. Babies are born and some of them grow up to be responsible men and women and some do not. Birth alone does not confer the right to self government, nor the right to band together in order to interfere with the management of another man's private business.

LANE
   You apparently dislike democracy a much as you do labor unions.
(grinds out cigarette in ash tray)

WILLHART
   Pure democracy is mob rule. Elections in a democratic society mean simply popularity contests that elevate mediocre men to office.
(crosses back to sit on desk)
   I don't want to see this nation once more given license to the "have-nots" to exploit the "haves".

LANE
(moving toward center)
   Governor, I came here to discuss with you my party's legislative platform. Unless you propose to outlaw political parties as well, we expect to be the majority force in the legislative assembly. That is, when you decide to hold elections and allow a representative government to replace your "rubber stamp" ministerial council. You can't keep the lid on much longer. Our party represents a moderate approach to government. Accept our platform and allow a democracy once more and you will have our support.
(moves toward Willhart)
   On the other hand, deprive the people of the right to hold these elections and you'll soon be dealing with radical groups such as the Human Liberties Association, or the Communists and the very revolution that you want to suppress will be right on your doorstep.

WILLHART
(rising and moving toward Lane)
   I can't agree, Mr. Lane, that I must submit to a popularity contest just to avoid running afoul of the Communists, or some other radical group.

LANE
(facing Willhart directly)
Then, Governor, you are inviting a power struggle and, perhaps, even your own assassination. Sorry, but I can't support your dictatorship and must work all the harder for a democracy.

WILLHART
Thanks for your candor, Mr. Lane.
(extends right hand to Lane who shakes hands somewhat self-consciously)
I am sorry to lose your support, but you are not the first man to be repelled by my policies. I believe that you are making a mistake, but I appreciate your integrity.

(Lane nods slowly and reluctantly. The two men look each other directly in the eyes as they continue to shake hands.)

CURTAIN.

END SCENE TWO

SCENE THREE

SCENE:
One month later.

AT RISE:
A representative of the Human Liberties Association is addressing a street crowd composed of approximately twenty people, encircling the speaker's platform (UC) which he occupies. The SPEAKER is in his late twenties. He is tall, intellectual- looking, and neatly dressed. Crowd reacts to his comments and to comments of other listeners as well.

SPEAKER
So, fellow citizens, we now have a tyrant in the person of General Willhart heading our national government. A man who brought our civil war to an end and promised stable government has now established a brutal dictatorship in the form of a police state.

FIRST LISTENER
(UR)
He's brought about order and stability in the country, hasn't he? It's now safe to walk the streets.

SPEAKER
Sure, at the price of our civil liberties. There's order, all right. Why shouldn't there be? The army and the national police swarm all over the streets day and night. Mandatory identification cards and curfews allow them to breathe down our necks twenty-four hours a day. Our provisional criminal code is a reversion to barbarism. Look what he did to the labor unions. Unions have been dissolved and it's a violation of the law to belong to one. Any grievance a worker has must now be submitted on an individual basis directly to the

21

Labor Commission. How many workers are going to risk their jobs by complaining about their employer to a government agency?

FIRST LISTENER
Yeah, and there haven't been any violent strikes either and wages have never been so good and unemployment so low as under Willhart. All the unions ever accomplished was to raise prices for the consumer with their "feather bedding" and screaming for higher wages while the big shots were lining their pockets with dues money. Most working men aren't complaining about Willhart. They're too busy enjoying the greatest prosperity this nation's ever known.

SPEAKER
I guess you think his policies on censorship are adding to our prosperity as well, don't you? Ask publishers and booksellers how they're enjoying this great national economic prosperity. Get an opinion from writers, artists, filmmakers, or anybody in the entertainment industry. General Willhart has set himself up as moral and artistic arbiter of what the nation will see, read, and hear. His censorship policies have put freedom of creative expression in a bureaucratic strait-jacket.

SECOND LISTENER
(UL)
I don't hear any creative people of true ability complaining. Now at least we can let our kids walk down the street without seeing explicit sex displayed on the cover of some magazine in a book store window. We can take our families to the movies without having to listen to vulgar language. Furthermore, we don't have a lot of propaganda coming out of films and television now that they're no longer controlled by a small group of left wingers who distorted everything we saw and

heard. I believe we're getting the truth through the media now, though Willhart does resort to censorship.

SPEAKER

True! You may know enjoy a media distorted by the government rather than the left wingers to which you refer. Although you and I apparently have very different ideas about self expression, let me ask you a question. How do you feel about his policies on public education? All teachers in public schools must sign loyalty oaths to the government and must list all the organizations to which they've ever belonged as part of an inquisitorial application procedure. Censorship policies on literature for classroom use is ludicrous and, speaking of propaganda, textbooks must be sufficiently propagandized to suit the government. History courses are especially scrutinized so that nothing critical of our national heritage will be taught. Needless to say, the teachers are under constant surveillance by Willhart to assure that they toe the mark.

SECOND LISTENER

Well, pal, who pays the piper calls the tune. Why shouldn't any person who teaches our kids be thoroughly investigated before being turned loose in the classroom? You imply that there's a lot of propaganda in the teaching of our nation's history under Willhart. Well, the writing and teaching of history is largely a matter of interpretation. Our nation has a pretty admirable history and I'd rather err a little on the positive side, even if you call it propaganda, than have some bleeding heart up there badmouthing something that our ancestors did several generations ago.

SPEAKER

That's a good flag waving speech, but I can't see it appealing to anyone who truly believes in academic freedom. And speaking of freedom, where's the freedom promised to the slaves? They all expected immediate emancipation after peace was achieved and now look at the mess that Willhart has created.

THIRD LISTENER
(moving UR toward Speaker)
What mess? Freedom is available to any slave who wants to acquire it.

SPEAKER
Theoretically, yes, but hardly in practice. Slaves who become free are forced to leave the country. Sure, some other countries are willing to accept them as immigrants, but they aren't trained for any occupation other than slavery. They end up taking the most menial and lowest paying jobs in their new society, or else turn to petty crime. They still bear the stigma of having been slaves in our country. Turning out these people who were an iternal part of our nation is like emancipation a child and putting him out on the street to fend for himself.
(sarcastically)
It did mean jobs for our unemployed, of course.

THIRD LISTENER
Well, the program has been in operation only a few months, but emancipated slaves are still better off than their ancestors who came here in chains. Hell, every immigrant group starts off at the bottom of the social and economic ladder in the host country, but they don't have to stay there forever. I haven't heard about any of these slave emigres wanting to come back to their former owners.

SPEAKER
Probably not, for they couldn't return if they tried. These poor people were practically "tractored off the land". Most owners were glad to get rid of them in exchange for manumission payments with which they

could buy more farm machinery. The slaves never really had an option; their owners did.

THIRD LISTENER
Yet those who remained slaves do have absolute economic security and their children have a right to public education. Their standard of living is much better than that of starving millions in other parts of the world. Furthermore, we compensated the owners fairly for the slaves that were freed. There was no confiscation of property involved.

SPEAKER
Say what you will. A slave is still a slave. Under Willhart's scheme, they'll never be citizens of this country. Our dictator has some very restrictive ideas about just who should live in our new society. Look at his policy on immigration. His Naturalization Order makes entry into the country practically impossible. Only a few selected nations will be given immigration quotas. These nations, needless to say, are in Willhart's words, "ethnically and culturally cognate" to our own. The rest of the world will look at us as an ethnocentric society.

FOURTH LISTENER
(moving UL toward Speaker)
Well, we aren't out to run a popularity contest with the rest of the world. You know that the surest way to fail is by trying to please everybody, don't you? Right now we have no room, nor economic demand for immigrants. We aren't under any more obligation to open our country to unrestricted immigration than you are to open your home to more people than you can comfortably house.

SPEAKER
You can't evaluate a person's fitness to enter this country on a generalization such as his national origin.

FOURTH LISTENER

Perhaps not, but laws must deal with generalities if there's any hope of enforcing them. Only nations with homogeneous populations have shown much progress in the modern world. Look at history. Diverse languages, cultures, and religions have led only to revolutions, "scapegoating", and the loss of national power. Look at the problems that unrestricted immigration has caused in other countries.

SPEAKER

Well, if it's uniformity you want, Willhart's your man. His immigration policy is bad enough, but the proposed birth control program is even worse. Limiting the number of children that any woman may have is as pernicious an interference with human rights as a government could possibly impose on its citizens. It interferes with religious beliefs as well as the God given biological process. Man is now playing God!

FOURTH LISTENER

Man's been playing at being God ever since he learned to cook meat over a fire. There's only so much space and fertility on this old planet and the way the world's population has been increasing for the past two centuries, if we don't interfere with nature, our descendants will be going to war against one another to see who eats and who doesn't. Governments must limit the number of people born if we're to survive. Who else can or will?

SPEAKER

Our nation is not one where people are crowding each other into the streets. Besides, how can such a law be enforced? Imagine a woman's being prosecuted as a criminal for having a third child!

FIFTH LISTENER
(moving UR)
No, our nation is not so crowded as some others in the world, but the more enlightened nations have to show the way. Wander through the street of any large city in the world and observe all the people who never should have been born; people who were unwanted children and were simply a burden to their parents. Many were from poor families of ten or twelve children and were raised in poverty by and older brother or sister, or given to a relative like an unwanted animal. They never had a chance in life, but they still grew up to breed like rodents just as their parents did before them. How do you enforce the law, you say? We make it like an other appropriate criminal statute, a deterrent. In a law and order society like ours, that term is not just a word on a page.

SPEAKER
Oh, yeah? Wait until all the concealed births begin to take place and babies become black market items. Then you'll see how well our deterrent works, or how well you reduce the number of the quote, "people who should have never been born."

FIFTH LISTENER
Once the people become oriented toward limited parenthood, it won't be so hard. Remember, there will be dispensations whereby certain married couples may have more than two children if they wish. Some can even qualify for the privilege of having an unlimited number of offsprings, if they can meet the necessary financial, educational, and genetic requirements.

SPEAKER
Yes, exactly. These "special dispensations" make the program all the more obnoxious. Discrimination in human birth is what we'll have along with a caste system

where some people are encouraged to reproduce, some allowed to do so, and others prohibited. How can any society make such an encroachment on the individuals's human right?

5TH SPEAKER
Well, if it makes for a better society, what's wrong with it?

SPEAKER
Yes, better, according to Willhart's values. Listen, birth restriction is only the beginning. Reliable rumors are now circulating that a full-scale Eugenics program is in the offing. Soon we'll be faced with sterilization, human experimentation, and "stud farms", all programmed to produce a super race.

SIXTH LISTENER
(moving UL)
What would be so bad about that? A nation is simply a product of its people, isn't it? If we regulate who comes into the country and who are born into it, won't we gradually become a superior people?

SPEAKER
Is it a superior society that sterilizes some of its members and sees to it that they will never know the experience of producing an offspring? If so, I want no part of it!

SIXTH LISTENER
The highest courts of the most enlightened countries of the world have upheld the validity of sterilization laws. How else can a society protect itself from misfits with undesirable hereditary traits?

SPEAKER
Again, I ask, who shall determine what traits are undesirable? General Willhart? Start out with the

feeble-minded and next we're sterilizing anybody who acts a little eccentric or who doesn't measure up physically to Willhart's idea of a superman. Next, we'll have compulsory euthanasia for anyone who's getting too old, or who doesn't have the right complexion for the new society.

SIXTH LISTENER
Now, you're twisting everything out of prospective. Willhart is not about to prescribe mercy killings for a lot of old people and you know it. But, concerning your question as to who will decide what genetic traits are undesirable, why not hereditary health court composed of doctors and psychiatrists? A planned program of sterilization doesn't have to be conducted on a 'hit or miss' basis, does it?

SPEAKER
No, it doesn't, and the fact that it won't is the very thing that I fear. Pretty soon only the super humans will be having the children and with the aid of pseudo-scientific gadgetry to assure a perfect breed.

SIXTH LISTENER
Why shouldn't we have a Eugenics program? Selective breeding produces superior animals. Why can't it produce superior human beings? Encouraging selected men and women to reproduce could have great benefits for our society. Galton made that observation over a century ago.

SPEAKER
How do you determine a superior human being? It's easy enough among animals when you're thinking in terms of faster horses,or beefier cattle, but it's not that simple when you come to the species of man. Do you want muscle men or math geniuses?

29

SIXTH LISTENER

I'd say that, ideally, we try and combine the two. However, if that approach is not practical, then you create both types according to society's mission. Not every child need be a potential Flash Gordon or Wonder Woman, but all may be free of genetic birth defects. Selective mating of slaves in former societies produced some superior physical types. No reason why we couldn't accomplish the same.

SPEAKER

So we breed men and women like animals and create a super race? Take no account of sentimental things such as love and marriage, but just force them to copulate and produce a super national breed?

SIXTH LISTENER

Hold on now! That's not the way a Eugenics program works. It's main emphasis is simply in preventing birth defects. Nobody would be forced into a marriage, nor would there be encouragement to mate outside the marital bond. The government would simply educate its citizens to be Eugenics conscious and would try to promote through youth programs marriages among the young people best qualified to be parents. They would be encouraged to wed, but hardly forced to do so.

SPEAKER

Assuming then that we have a nation of superior humans, what do we do with them? Go out and conquer all our inferior neighboring nations? With all these geniuses and test tube concocted muscle men and perfectly molded women, won't there be a struggle to see which set will dominate the other? Or will the combined traits in the potential philosopher kings allow that class to dominate both? Isn't it going to be a bit dull without a few poor slobs around to lord it over in such an elite society? Who's going to do all the menial labor, or am I forgetting that we'll still have the contented voluntary slave class for that purpose? No, thanks. I want no part of a genetic "New Deal". I'll take my chances in a free society, not a biologically structured "stud farm" in a police state.

SEVENTH LISTENER
There you go again with that police state label. If this is such a suppressed society, then how do you figure that you and your Human Liberties Association fellows can get up and make such speeches as you're doing now? I haven't seen any uniformed bullies out here clubbing you over the head.

SPEAKER
No, but I'm sure that everything that I've said will be reported to Willhart. He has tabs on all who want to force liberal ideas on his regime.

SEVENTH LISTENER
Well, you Human Liberties Association fellows are always looking out for the underdog and trying to see that everyone gets your brand of social justice, but I believe all you really accomplish is the stirring up of one class against another and the undermining of authority. Democracy works fine when you have nothing too important to decide and plenty of time to debate the issues, but when it comes to critical matters, the process is just too slow. Somebody like Willhart had to take action and save the nation and it doesn't matter whether you call him a dictator, a tyrant or a savior.

SPEAKER
(becoming more emotional)
He's been saving us from disorder for over a year now and the people have not yet had one word of say in the conduct of the government. His only advice comes from his military 'toadies' on the Council of Ministers, a rubber stamp kitchen cabinet posing as a legislative

council. There will never be a representative government so long as Willhart's in power. Popular soverenignty will ge a dream. If voting is ever allowed, it will be only on a highly restricted basis.

SEVENTH LISTENER
Why should everyone have the right to vote? Those who want a say in running society should first have some stake in society. Otherwise, you have nothing but mob rule. I understand that Governor Willhart plans to hold elections within the next six months, but only the qualified will be allowed to vote.

SPEAKER
And who are these "qualified"? Those who accept the necessity of a dictatorship for law and order?

SEVENTH LISTENER
According to the news media, all citizens over twenty-one will be allowed to apply for a voting permit. Property ownership, net worth, educational background, stable employment, reputation of character, and the ability to pass a written citizenship test will all be considered in granting the privilege. We'll have an electorate all right, and it will be a responsible one.

SPEAKER
You forgot to add so long as the applicant has not been a rabble rouser or a member of a dangerous liberal organization. Anything the news media says is altered to Willhart's approval. Even if the media is correct, I don't call an oligarchy a form of popular sovereignty. Governments that don't trust the people have no right to ask the people to trust them. We've got a military dictatorship under Willhart now and there isn't going to be any real change. There may be a pretext of representative government with a token legislature and even a mock constitution, but the real power will remain centered in one man. However,

32

Governor Willhart, or General Willhart, should remember the frequent fate of tyrants. He's encouraging another rebellion and if he meets with a violent end, he has only himself to blame.

(TWO UNIFORMED SOLDIERS, or national policemen, enter from left and walk directly to Speaker's platform.)

FIRST POLICEMAN
All right, pal, you've said enough. Your comments are beginning to sound like treason and you're encouraging violent crime. You'd better come with us.

SPEAKER
(stepping down from the platform)
How can I be guilty of treason against a government which I never had any say in establishing? Nevertheless, I will come along.

(SPEAKER is escorted off stage right by the TWO POLICEMEN. Members of crowd watch and continue to talk among themselves.)

CURTAIN

END SCENE THREE

SCENE FOUR

SCENE:
Two weeks later. Living room of the Presidential mansion occupied by the WILLHARTS. It is a large room filled with fashionable sofa and two sitting chairs.

AT RISE:
WILLHART, wearing his dress uniform, enters from left. He is carrying a briefcase.
ELIZABETH, his wife, follows him. She is an attractive, willowy blonde approximately forty years old. She is wearing a house dress.

ELIZABETH
John, please be careful on the streets this morning. I've been so tense this past week with all the radical agitation against your program.

WILLHART
(stops UC and faces Elizabeth)
Nothing to worry about, love. I've got tight personal security and the whole army to look out after me, haven't I?

ELIZABETH
Even so, I don't like the idea of your exposing yourself to the crowds. It only takes one fool assassin to kill you or any other government leader. Please don't get out on the streets so much.

WILLHART
(sets briefcase on floor, puts both hands on her shoulders)
Don't even think about those possibilities. I got through the war without a scratch, didn't I? I can't run the government from my office all of the time, love. I

just have to accept some of the hazards of being the military strongman that some like to call me.

ELIZABETH
    I know, but that doesn't make it any easier for me. You've accomplished so much for the nation already, John. Isn't it time to let up a little and make some concession to the radicals, as you call them?

WILLHART
    Not yet, Liz.
(picks up briefcase)
    I've got to hold on tightly for a few more months or risk undoing everything we've worked so hard for up to this point.
(takes Elizabeth's right hand in his left)
    Then we can afford to loosen up and talk about a new Constitution.

ELIZABETH
    You're idealistic, John, and stubborn, but don't go and get yourself killed over a political issue. Don't wait too long to "loosen up". I'm afraid your enemies may be growing impatient.

WILLHART
    My driver probably is as well. Goodbye, love.
(kisses her on forehead)
    Must be going.

(WILLHART exits to right. ELIZABETH watches him apprehensively. Slowly moves to sofa and sits.)

CURTAIN.

ANNOUNCER (O.S.)
(off stage before curtain)
We interrupt our regularly scheduled program to regretfully inform you that Governor Willhart has been assassinated. The Governor was struck by bullets fired by two gunmen from a passing car as he was entering a limousine in front of the Presidential mansion at approximately 9:30 this morning. Governor Willhart was pronounced dead on arrival at Highland Park Hospital. The two assassins are believed to be members of a radical revolutionary organization.

END SCENE FOUR

SCENE FIVE

SCENE:
Same setting several hours later that day.

AT RISE:
ELIZABETH is seated on the sofa, UC.
GENERAL JAMES CROWLEY is seated in the chair to her right. He is approximately the same age and physical appearance as Willhart and is wearing a dress uniform.

ELIZABETH
(stoically)
I knew it would be only a matter of time until it happened. John brought it on himself. Somehow he seemed to think that he was invulnerable to assassination. Couldn't he see that it would take only one deranged radical to wipe out a man who ignored the demands of the demagogues?
(pauses)
Who killed him, Jim?

CROWLEY
Two members of a radical revolutionary group, probably with Communist ties. Both are in custody now and already playing the "martyr to ending tyranny" roles.
(pauses)
At least our courts will never listen to a criminal insanity plea.
(rising and moving down right)
Why the hell didn't we have closer security along the street!?

ELIZABETH
(stoically)
It would have happened sooner or later, regardless of security.

(rising and moving toward Crowley)
Well, if these two killers consider themselves martyrs, what do they think they've made of John? Surely most of the nation will appreciate what he's accomplished during the past fourteen months. Will someone else continue where he left off, or have the spokesmen for popular sovereignty made their point once and for all by murdering my husband?

CROWLEY
(turning to face Elizabeth)
Elizabeth, there's a revolutionary spirit within every nation that is as hard to resist as the ocean's tide. Dissatisfied elements emerge, grow, and overthrow one power by revolution and replace it with another. The people are never any better off after these revolutions, but the propagandists try to convince them otherwise.

ELIZABETH
And the people believe those propagandists who argue that pure democracy is the only justifiable form of government.

CROWLEY
(pacing about down stage and to sofa, UC)
So they do. Next comes the mob to protest, demonstrate,thwart progress, and create more chaos by opposing the very leaders they've elected to office. People get impatient and, perhaps, another dictatorship now comes into power to be violently replaced by another revolutionary tide of democracy and on and on the circle goes.
(sits on sofa)

ELIZABETH
Do you believe John's assassination will bring about another revolution?

CROWLEY
    I hope not, but unless someone can quickly fill John's shoes, I'm afraid another one is inevitable.

ELIZABETH
(moving to chair, UR)
    Won't the demagogues start demanding a new Constitution and a return to popular government, now that they've eliminated John?

CROWLEY
    I'm sure they will, and, speaking of tyranny, we'll have it. I mean, tyranny of the majority; the worst form of tyranny possible. The majority in any society is a majority of incompetents. The people vote according to selfish and emotional motives. Elections are a popularity contest in which those who can appeal to the whims of the mob emerge as winners. So the government then rotates on the axis of popularity, demagoguery, and the threat of exploitation of the "haves" by the "have nots".

ELIZABETH
    How can a society counteract these forces?
(sits in chair, UR)

CROWLEY
    Through the will and power of a single strong leader.
(moving down stage)
    All the democratic debate over issues accomplishes nothing until that one "hero on horseback" emerges and makes things happen. It doesn't matter whether you call him king, president, protector, or even dictator. So long as he has the power at the opportune time. John Willhart was that hero! He was implementing a sound program of progress for this nation. He knew much better that the people themselves what was good for them and most of them

realized it. Yet, now he's dead because he wouldn't seek approval from the masses for everything he did!

ELIZABETH
You don't believe that democracy will work in any society?

CROWLEY
A limited democracy such as John envisioned for us can work. He was willing to allow those qualified have a vote, but the liberals and the Human Liberties Association would never accept anything less than universal suffrage. They and the Communists constantly portrayed him as a brutal despot and stirred up resentment against him.
(sits on sofa)
Look at history, Elizabeth. Cromwell, Napoleon, Jackson, Lincoln, Theodore Roosevelt were all men who resorted to direct action, and by-passed the democratic legislative process. What would they have achieved if they had always waited on legislative approval instead of acting on their own initiative?

ELIZABETH
(moving to sofa beside Crowley)
Yes, but those men were all war mongers, either directly or indirectly. Jim, the nation needs another "hero on horseback" at this very moment to promote peace, not war. You know you were John's choice as a successor from the start. He always had great confidence in you as an Army officer and as a member of his Council of Ministers. The Council will name you as First deputy to be Military Governor. Are you willing to assume the responsibility of carrying on John's work . . . and the risk?

CROWLEY
(deliberately)
I want to think about it, Elizabeth.

(pause)

I want to be sure that I'm capable of handling power, as John did.

(almost to himself)

Also, I want to be sure that I'm willing to become another martyr if necessary. You pose a question that is not easily answered.

ELIZABETH
(rising)

Jim, I can't be a Spartan any longer. I need to be alone. I'm leaving the funeral plans to you. Think and pray long and hard, or else John Willhart will be this nation's "last hero".

(CROWLEY rises and bows his head slightly as ELIZABETH begins to sob quietly and exits left. Slowly, he kneels in prayer.)

CURTAIN.

END SCENE FIVE

END ACT ONE

THE END.

<u>Biographical Sketch: Jerry Patterson</u>

Jerry Patterson is a native of Arkansas, a Harvard man, and a current resident of the San Fernando Valley of southern California where he has enjoyed moderate success as a lawyer, actor, writer, and teacher.

He holds a Doctor of Jurisprudence degree from Vanderbilt University and was a Rotary Fellow to the University of Sydney (Australia) in 1961. Mr. Patterson is also a former Assistant Attorney General of Arkansas. During the 1950's he served as a Company Commander with the Eighth U.S. Army in Korea.